Time for Bed, Fred!

YASMEEN ISMAIL

WALKER BOOKS FOR YOUNG READERS
AN IMPRINT OF BLOOMSBURY
NEW YORK   LONDON   NEW DELHI   SYDNEY

Bong Bong Bong Bong Bong Bong Bong Bong Bong

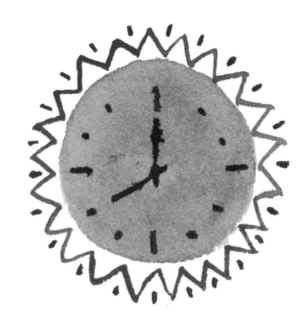

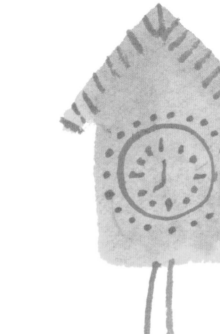

It's time for bed, Fred!

Oh no, Fred,
where are you going?

Fred?

That's not your bed, Fred!

Fred?
What are you doing
up there?

Trees are no places
for dogs.

UH-OH!

Where's your bed, Fred?

Fred!

Fred!

Fred!

Watch out for the **muddy puddle . . .**

Too late!
Oh, Fred, you are **filthy.**

Bath time!

Wait, Fred, wait!

You're not dry yet.

Oh dear!

Come on, Fred.
It's time for bed.

Fred?

Fred?

Fred?

It's **very** late now, Fred.
Time for bed.

Okay, you can have a story first.
But just one.

Now, where's your bed, Fred?

That's not your bed, Fred!

That's not your bed, Fred!

That's not YOUR bed, Fred!

Oh, Fred, that's MY bed!
Let's find your bed, Fred . . .

At last!

Night-night, Fred.
Sweet dreams!

For Alasdair

First published in Great Britain in July 2013 by Bloomsbury Publishing Plc
Published in the United States of America in February 2014 by Walker Books for Young Readers, an imprint of Bloomsbury Publishing, Inc.
www.bloomsbury.com

For information about permission to reproduce selections from this book, write to
Permissions, Walker BFYR, 1385 Broadway, New York, New York 10018
Bloomsbury books may be purchased for business or promotional use. For information on bulk purchases please contact
Macmillan Corporate and Premium Sales Department at specialmarkets@macmillan.com

Library of Congress Cataloging-in-Publication Data
Ismail, Yasmeen, author, illustrator.
Time for bed, Fred! / Yasmeen Ismail.
pages   cm
Summary: A child has a very difficult time getting Fred, the dog, to bed.
ISBN 978-0-8027-3597-3 (hardcover) • ISBN 978-0-8027-3598-0 (reinforced)
[1. Dogs—Fiction. 2. Bedtime—Fiction.] I. Title.
PZ7.I83833Tim 2014   [E]—dc23   2013010711

Art created with watercolors • Typeset in Bernhard Gothic • Book design by Zoe Waring

Printed in China by C&C Offset Printing Co., Ltd., Shenzhen, Guangdong
2 4 6 8 10 9 7 5 3 1 (hardcover)
2 4 6 8 10 9 7 5 3 1 (reinforced)